For Yamoah Family

Every word written in ink are words spoken with tongue,
for words speaks language of the mind.

Kofi Yamoah

A Collection of Words with Emotions

In his eyes

In his eyes
Redness symbolises pain, as blood streams from veins upon
earths ground . . . poppies blossom with every taste.

In his eyes
Only rain can complement tears
For when it rains it pours like tear drops.

In his eyes
The future has never been bright
But pitch black like the night without the moon.

A dreamer's dream can fulfil all hope
But the dreams he foresee is filled with nightmares.

In his eyes
It's a daily struggle of survival
For hunger strikes by the minute
And the river dries by the season.

Shelter must be a luxury,
For those who sleep beneath them, us they gain a good sleep,
but soft beds are figments of his imagination.
In his eyes

The hardness of grounds
Depicts the pits in which a casket is laid to rest
For above the surface, he must lay his head to sleep and sleep
is the cuisine of DEATH!

In his eyes
To believe in faith
There must be a God who bears witness to all things living.

The road to heaven is a stretch and people can never be judges
on judgement day, but witnesses in his eyes!

Through these eyes the world is a mere pain to true dreams,
for reality has never been kind but unfair.

In his eyes, there's no sight of innocent but a struggle to live by
any means necessary.

These eyes . . .
In his eyes.

War games

A game of war
The flashes of lights
With the sounds of guns
Rains down fire balls of punishment
The gloomy skies may glow with anger
With ashes of smoke flakes down like powder
Cries of the innocent, silent but deadly
Corpses of babies never led no life
Mothers in pain pour out emotions
A time of war is the need of survival.

Blinded by tears

Please, don't shed tears!
Nor cry out in secret, for I am here by your side
To dry one's eyes and mend your shattered heart
Though I bear a broken heart, I shall endure such pain
alongside your falling tears.

Blinded by tears such a word like love is a mystery and bares
so much misery, yet filled with happy moments.

Although we both bid farewell to our bleeding hearts, we shall
soon embrace love in the pursuit of happiness.

So please don't shed tears while you seek out new life.

Awake

Awake from this forgotten sleep of nightmare in blood for your eyes shatters in the fear of darkness and reeks with hatred.

Alone but not forgotten
You dream of a lustful day, only to receive half empty cup.

A better day could be round the corner
Bow down your head and pray for a happy day,
For tomorrow could be your last.

Awake, awake, awake . . .

City of lights

The city of lights!
Don't shine with natural born sunlight
The sun may shine at day but at night,
The skies glow with sparks of colours.

The light of red,
Shines like flames
The light of yellow,
Blossom like sunflower
The light of green,
Is as green as grass
While the light of blue,
Is as clear as the clear blue skies.

The city that never sleeps,
Is the city that party all night.

City of VEGAS,
Is the city of lights!

Cry

Why must you cry?
If there be pain, don't shed tears of sorrow
Nor cry out in misery.

Bear the pain; hold back your falling tears
Don't make it RAIN, pouring out your emotions in a well of
wishes.

Be more like a man with pride and don't shed painful tears
alone in the emptiness of darkness.

Hold down your emotions shred it deep within the books you
read and pour out sparks of stars with each tear drop, cry no
more.

Caged man

Trapped like a rat,
With no place to hide,
Caged like a bird whistling songs of sorrow.

Held captive for a sinners mind,
Your criminal intentions got you caged like an animal.

To repent is to be free or to lead the life of a caged man?

Breathless, gasping for a pinch of air in this God forsaken cage.

Nightfall brings no comfort,
Yet the dark reeks with nothing but fear and tears.

Wishing to be set free just to inhale fresh air of freedom, will it
ever be as fresh as snow or as filthy as the ghetto gutters?

The life of a caged man filled with misery,
Never to be caged like a bird, but to be set free like a white dove.

Freedom at last

In a hell hole
You were placed in captivity
Like a jail bird
Nowhere to go
No freedom of air
They wished to demise your soul,
Vanquish your political views
Captured for the games of politics you played
Those flying the flags of power wanted to silent your political aims

Caged like a bird and out of sight
21years held in a hell hole, for darkness to swallow you whole.

Hope must have kept you strong,
Freedom came out the blue to walk among men, women and children.

Freedom at last,
Free from chains,
Captivity no longer a prison but with freedom, you broke free from deaths grasp.

Set a goal to be the follower
A leader in a falling country,
A survivor among broken men,
An inspiration to all nations,
A freedom fighter that will forever last.

Freedom at last!
Freedom at last!
Freedom at last!

Loneliness

Whenever light falls
The night is silent
Where ever there's love
There shall be loneliness
If there be a tear drop from a lonely heart,
Let it bear one wish . . . 'to find true love'.

The path of loneliness, witness more misery than a grave yard without caskets and all hearts grieve for the joy of comfort, just like all dead souls crave for a bright light!

Loneliness is more than isolation,
Loneliness is sanity without a companion,
Loneliness is a blind man without sight travelling through space, 'lonely'.

What is loneliness to you?

Success

Strive through success,
And all heart's desires shall follow
From the riches of money making,
Will develop to pleasures of accessories

The rich and powerful always prevail,
While those in poverty fight for a chance to succeed.

Depend on the ability of your skills,
Work your heart out to achieve your goals.

Set your mind upon success and allow determination to drive you towards your one true wish, because success can only bear its true fruit with pure CONFIDENCE!

Determination is an attribute that stands strong between failing souls, and if there be failure as success seems to be out of reach, cast all shame aside and try again.

If you try and don't succeed, try, try again and embrace the motto of never giving up.
Succeed and keep head tilt to the skies,
For the skies shall be the ultimate success.

Politics

<u>Dedicated to my father</u>

Politics is a pulse through all veins,
But my father possess the knowledge and understanding
beyond the mind of a politician.

Politics is like a rush that's hard to expose until the truth is
revealed, all politics bear many lies and corruption.

But to be a politician, you must share words among those who
vote for the people have the power to elect and eliminate.

Be true to yourself,
Be true to the people,
Be the best politician,
Be the right politician,
Allow the truth to be your speech therapy, and lead by example.

To be heard is to be seen,
For popularity shall be your crown.

Politics is the key to society,
The rules of humanity,
For those in charge are creators of the law
Like the Ten Commandments was written in stone, humanities
laws are written in ink upon a leaf of paper.

Decisions made across nation's bears its tongue through debates of politics.

But what does it take to be a politician?

Trust must be a factor,
Confidence must bear boldness,
Loyalty is inevitable in the eyes of voters, and promises must forever be kept!

Fly high

Be a bird,
Grow some wings,
For the sky is in need of a fly.

Fly high, higher than mountain Fuji
Don't buzz like a bee for you alone make the morning whisper
with sounds of melody.

You dance along with the spills of rain like the first fall of
leaves at autumn.

You alone can bond with the skies like birds fly among
angels.

They say what goes up must come down,
Yet you belong with the stars like the solar system.

So let your feet bear wings and soar higher than birds between
clouds and the moon.

Paint your own picture and escape among flies like birds
migrating through skies.

Fly then fly some more like there's no limit to the winds pane
of your wings.
Make your mark beyond the stars and splash out your name
among the god's of light, fly high.

Her red hair

The sky is blue,
Roses are red,
Her fairy-tale hair attracts the glow of the sun.

The nature of her hair compliments the roots of beetroots; she is by far the beauty of a red rose for she smells as sweet as a flower.

Her natural red hair blooms of colours of a rainbow but never has she been forsaken by her true beauty.

Her appearance resembles the goddess of attraction and the lady with the red colours floating in her hair depicts nature's vivid spring rose.

She imitates the goddess of purity, and if images of perfection is achievable then her alone mirror perfection in its physical form.

She captured beauty in its human form reflecting through all mirrors that shine.

The night

The night falls,
The night sleeps,
The night's dark,
The night's lonely,
The night's silent,
The night sparks with the glitz of many stars.

The mist of the night can cause a shiver,
The sounds of the night can cause a fright,
The night peaks once the day sleeps,
So night, night and sleep tight as you travel along the cross
roads of nightly dreams, goodnight and sleep well.

Silent night

Night after night tears keep pouring,
Mama sheds tears alongside the rain drops,
Papa keeps shouting, yet the house seems silent.

Tear drops upon tear drops flakes down my twine brown eyes,
while my blood boils in rage of such pain and anxiety.

What must I do to end such pain?
This pain too painful, such pain so awful,
The pain unbearable, so I suffer in silence.

Nothing but the rhythm of my heart beat
Can be heard through the barriers of my ear drums.

As I wipe away these tears that continues to fall,
I reminisce upon the days that smiles and laughter bounced
between the walls of our home like ping pong.

Silent night but there's a deep scream that pleads for sound,
like a tree that falls with no ear to catch its trembling crash.

Question, do I make a sound among witnessing eyes?

Lost in grief

The wild unforgettable night,
Clutter with pleasurable misery.

The thought of the lady is nothing more than a distant memory;
never will she set sight upon yesterday's unending moments.

Shall I review those intimate invitations that led to so much
flirtation and romance?

Those lips, with that kiss
Mmm, let's not forget those touches of raw goose bumps.

If only those eyes could see once more,
What will they appear to see?

Will they grieve with tears or glow with joy?

This is pleasurable memory, but why does this salty taste sink
down my cheek like sea water?

Am I lost in the grief of pain?
As I reminisce upon the wonderful days we shared, when she
wore my heart on her love finger.

Could this be broken heart am witnessing or the grief of letting
go of the one I once loved?

Tears licks the cheeks that once met the warmth of a lover's kiss, it's true what they say; you only miss the one you love once they are gone.

Since you been gone grief is a nightly night time story and rain proceeds to flee my eyes like raindrops escaping the skies.

Am lost in grief, so lost that I can no longer see,
But these ears that attract your voice can still hear whispers of your name . . .

Must I

Why must I weep in shame while my eyes pour at night?

The tears that I shed slip down my tender cheeks are never warm or sweet, is as cold as the icy snow that falls in winter.

Must I be known for who I am or to be seen for what I am in secret?

I am far from failure, in the process of success and happiness I smile with a smile.

Must I succeed to be proud?
Will I ever win a winners heart or to be more like a weeping heart?

I doubt my ability to be a success, yet there's no way I shall allow tears to run free in shame.

I will smile with my head held high,
So I shall do all that my brain can contain and achieve my goals.

For with words at the tip of my pen, I will open the eyes of the young to read and write and achieve the unachievable.

9

I reminisce in pain,
I cry in tears,
I laugh with a smile,
My heart ache with passion,
The pain thighs apart the love I bear deeply.

When will the pain I bear be replaced by the love we all seek?

Am I to be gunned down like a falling soldier or set alight by the flames of purity?

Blinded by the fair beauty of a graceful lady . . . will my tears seize to exist in moments of joy or only shed drops in times of misery?

I am, who I am and tears shall pour during painful days and smiles shall replace frowns on a happy day.

This is I, this is me.

Imperfect man

MAN?!
A word consumed with POWER
Adored by the grace of women
Protector of those hopeless,
Yet why are we so imperfect?!
We bare so much affection and love
But the arrogance and pride of imperfect man, over shadows
our caring heart.

Perfection

We may not be perfect
But we do crave perfection
In the search of success,
We rise above the rest,
We may be imperfect but we only human.
What is PERFECTION?
Definition, flawless beyond recognition!

They say perfection is unachievable, then why does our soul
seek for companionship to feel complete?

In this world we all pieces to a puzzle, perfection is the image
that cradles in our eyes like a dream.

Nothing is unachievable,
Never give up the dream for if you dream it, you can turn
dreams to reality.

So bear fruit to your inner perfection.

The best

The best of the best,
Always walk on the best of lines,
Never lay their eyes off the wining prize.

Picture a world competition is a must, for the price is fame.

The world knows your name, no longer are you alone to walk
in the streets unknown.

The best of the best,
Never back down from a challenge,
Like a cat, chasing its mouse.

What must it take to be the best?
For I too, want to be the best, and walk among the best of the
best.

Night hunter

As the night creeps among daylight,
I seek out my spear to quench my heroic taste.
I am a man among many men, but a hunter without a prey.

Night hunter without eyes to view the world I walk on daily.

My senses my ears, the trigger of sounds the earth makes is my music.

No longer, am I a child trapped in a box without sight but a night hunter transformed to survive in this ghostly world of survival.

Born and nurtured, not by nature but by the daily hunt of life.

Can you see what I see?

Can you see what I see?
The pride of an African man
Toppling obstacles placed in the way of his misfortune.

Can you feel what he feels?
The sorrow buried deep within the depth of his lonely heart.

Can you see what I see?
The seed growing deep within the natural soil of African land,
nurtured by the very hands of many men and women.

This is what I see, but can you see what I see?

Killing me softly

Gone . . .
But not forgotten,
Hands as soft as yours, can no longer mend my aching wounds.

You pieced those timid eyes within a soul
As flourish as mine and bleed me dry.
Those joyous days that bloomed with smiles and laughter, no
longer does my twin eyes close to picture a dreamful dream.

Drained and heartless, left with floods of tears to endure such
pain.

To kill a heart this pure and still not weeps,
You alone can cause so much grief.

No longer do you share the same heart we once discovered,
but by bleeding me dry am constantly reminded by these scares
imprinted around me like tattoos.

You killed me, patiently with no passion blossom in your eyes,
yet tears did sprung down your cheeks like running water
Though I still wonder, why are you killing me softly?

She weeps

The tears that pour down her eyes, tears of desperation
Redemption reeks from her appealing skin like a ripped apple
I sleep with thee, because she's in need of comfort,
Between my arms is where she rest her head to sleep

She's no angel, and neither am I
Because we all sinners by birth,
Cleansed by the purified water

When she does weep at night,
I cry along with the tears that crawl down her cold cheeks

The nightmare dreams of regret
That frights her fragile soul,
Determines the tears that drops down her silky pillow,
So when she does weep of pain,
She glows with such innocent beauty like a new born baby

As she weeps her pain away, she cleanse her sinful soul,
To rid the burden of mistakes trapped in her past.

Stormy nights are the worst nights,
For she shed more tears than the rain that pours,
But she's never been a weepier
Only to shred the tragic pain trapped in her unstable heart, so
she weeps.

Till this day

Till this day, am no longer known as your husband
For I lost the right and dignity to be tagged by such a word like 'man'
Ripping your heart apart was neither, through the passion of love
Nor in the heat of sex,
The grief of sadness, lit my awful lips to speak of all the painful memories that once torn your heart to shred
Your fibs alone open up an old wound that was forgotten in a locked cage
Am no longer afraid to cry out all the pain bottled up within, because you opened up a flood of tears once you walked away in the arms of another
Till this day I no longer weep,
But allow tears to run down my lips for life!

Red rose

The red rose
Bears its beauty from earths rich soil
Their root alone feeds on the sweetest taste of mineral water

The red rose
Love most admired gift
A flower famous for its sensational smell
That melts the hearts of Gods most adored creations, woman.

Yellow rose

The friendship rose, is the yellow rose
Its smell of fragrant differs from loves most treasured flower,
red rose
Its uniqueness blossom during the spring time season,
As it shines like the sun flower
Just like a friendship that last forever,
The sweetest smell of yellow rose lingers its natural beauty
during summer time.

Speak of me

Speak of me as you know me now
Not as am known by my past
My dear love, did we not vow to devour lies and only breathe
truth from our lips?
Why did you speak in such words that hunt my anger knowing
my hands are weapons of torture!

Speak of me as you know me now
Not as am known by my past
Yet for truth be told, you fear me like death
But your heart still bears unconditional love

Never will you allow your feet to defeat your heart
Knowing such love can withstand any pain inflicted
Share with me the passion that made your stomach float with flies,
So when I do speak in words such as these
Refer to me as you know me now, not as you once feared me
in the past

Remember the nights that stars became the glare in your eyes
And star gazing was more than our wishing well?
The sounds of the wind was more like the echoes of the sea
breeze, that sung a tune to our soothing ears

There are times my eyes catches your own and time itself
becomes the mere motion that ticks in silence.
Never forgetting the moment we met and the days we shared
continued to stream in a fluent motion like days of our lives
As words form speech and roll from your tongue,
Let it embrace, sentences of passion and speak of me as you
know me now.

Cupid strikes

I know not what you seek for
Yet I feel the need to be with you
Just when I thought love has forsaken me
Cupid strikes me with the arrows of affection and connection
Wow, what a crush!

The dream kiss

In dreams, I picture the softest touch of lips
With the sweetest taste of kisses
Once her lips meet mine, my dream shall be complete
This is the dream my heart wishes to fulfil at first sight
The fulfilment of this dream will be a wish come true.

Heartache

My heartaches,
Yet I feel no pain, I feel joy
Just buzzing like a bee
I cry tears, but my tears taste salty
In search of a love, I can never seem to find
I bear passion, as sweet as passion fruit
Am surrounded by love, and with my arms embrace it like a bear.

Me time

I need me time
I need the time to chill
I need the time to reminisce on the good times
With the bad times, this is not all times
Just night times, dream time, not day dream
Simply my time!

A poem

This is a poem, never a love note nor a music melody,
These words straight out of my heart and tears,
I am not out to offend the opposite sex,
Am simply expressing my heart's desire

Definition of a heart-warming poem
Touches all those willing to understand,
A poem with emotion gashes out like the streamline of a falling
waterfall

My poems thoughts of my imagination,
My experience spilled through the very ink
I am the seeker seeking out the true definition of life
These are my poems, expressions of my inner heart emotions.

My

Africa my homeland
Art my gimmick
Poetry my emotions
Music my entertainment
Family my inspiration
Friends my mates
Language my words
Life my path
Love my passion
Success my quest
Pen my ink
Cloths my style
The world my home!

A man

The world's evil alone cannot hold me down
Against an attacker, I shall boldly hold my ground
Because am a man with pride
A man with a heart

At night alone I run with fright
As the shadows of dark plot their evil against an angel, as fly
like the birds that sing

A man with a hidden talent,
Will do all that is possible to share his seeds, to bear fruit
A man got to do, what a man got to do
And the willingness to paint a vivid picture for the next
generation

A poet paint pictures with words
A musician create music with instruments
An actor acts with a motion through emotions
A runner runs with feet and a singer sings with a voice
Yet a man works with hands, love with heart and provides for
the family
But a man is more of a man with a woman by his side.

Punishment

Punishment of a cold wind
Feeling like a cold cat
Skin hair stands tall
Bubble rush goose bumps
Almost froze up, looking like an ice-pole

Punish by the cold wind
Shivering like a rattle snake
In need of the sunlight
To vanquish this unbearable cold

Sunny day

On this sunny period of sunny times
My mind is hot like the streamline of holy water, pouring out my God given body.

When the sun beams its ever blazing heat, the world seeks for shades while I bear my skin to the glow of light.

As hot as I am shinning bright on this sunny day and there are blessings that may rain from clouds but there is heat that always makes the skin glow.

To my unborn child

Born within a day of true specialty
Your birth alone shall be the rebirth of peace
Upon a world of evil your name will rain through clouds like
a blessing

To my unborn child you hold the knowledge of your father
with a blessing that showers down through heavens gates; you
are a gift like no other, unique like a single star . . . so bright

Pieces of you are the purity that I alone never shared till my
seeds swim through your mother's womb

You were born to achieve, to succeed and surpass the legacy
of your father
Be all you can be, the best you can be
Allow knowledge to sink through your blood stream like the
flow of water

To my unborn child
Words shall be the ink of your tongue, speak with conviction
and walk with pride
Never allow anger to over cloud your judgement
And spread love with your heart, not with your mind
Believe in your strength, but never let your fist connect the skin
of a lady
See the bright light that shines in all God's children, and when
you are blessed,
Share with those you love dearly and give to those unfortunate

My father once told me "education is the key", so read when
night arrives
Write when pain brings you tears, write when love makes your
heart race, and write when joy makes you laugh

To my unborn child,
Life is a gift, so love life with no regret
Let truth walk with you like your trusted eyes
Never allow lies to violate the ever purity of your soul

Always do right, and when you are met by wrong, walk on the
right lane
Set your own goals and fulfil all the dreams that make you
smile . . .
Although life's path will never be smooth, make your dreams
come true and the hardest worker always achieve above the rest.

This is a letter to my unborn child.

Let it flow

Let it flow,
Along the mountains path
Flows the sweetest source of waterfall
A river that flows forever
Only exist in dreams
For the happiest of men
Also weep like rain on 'Remembrance Day'.

Remember,
Those nights you cried and the tears that poured
Reflected the saddest moments of your life

Remember,
Those days you wept
And the rain showered alongside every tear drop you shed
You let it flow, like a river that bears no boundaries

So when you do feel pain, and tears begin to shred its splashes
along your cheeks,
Let it flow for miles without an ending drop.

Tears of the world

The world in tears is not the tears that rain, but through the clouds is the cleansing of sins
The falling cries of our dying soldiers are fuelled with the devils touch of destruction.

A place called home is no longer safe to embrace joy, but to run from fear and depression.

Despite love and happiness, a burden we all share to for fill our hidden fantasies.

The world still cries with every falling raindrop, and shall continue once the rainbow brings calm.

These are the tears of the world.

The jump off

Along the buildings edge he stood like a bird ready to take flight among the night's stars

In his eyes flood of tears gashed out in a plunge of flashes like the spill of oil

The sky was gloom like the nightmare zone of hell, with an angel consumed by total darkness reaching out for his white light

Call of death creeps in its evil form like thundering clouds conquering the blue skies

This final jump shall end all miseries and failures, for a father who drunk life to sleep and never bonded with his son.

He leaps, as all life floats in circulation around him and let faith decide his final splash . . .

In the heat

She makes me shiver with overwhelming joy; the sweetness of her heavenly lips has never been too sweet or sour for my sensitive lips and tongue to taste.

She loves me for me, and there for me in the mist of painful heartache

With her voice so warm, makes the hair at the back of my neck stand tall like green grass

She makes me shed more tears of passion every time she whispers the melody of her drums within my ears

There are times she can't be perfect, yet with her by my side perfection is a mere mirror in her spitting image

There's an emotion when once heart beat for miles and mind constantly speaks her name

In the heat she can be wild and brings the pleasure out my body

She's more than the fire that burns like heart burn;
She is the heat that gets me warm when cold shivers walks on my skin, she is the heat within my flame, always lets it burn.

Word

Word!
Expression of the mind
Expression of the heart
Expression of the soul, is more than expression of the body,
and yet like paint imprinted on a white slate, word.

Words, poetic verses of a romantic poem
Laid out among a rhythm of sentences
Words can be words among many words like the sound of
music echoing the core of the heart beat.

Words are the bond of speech, for the lips speak in tongue and
delivered through mouth, 'words'.

My love with words is my ambition to succeed, because
success is the channel to the path of open doors like the key
to unlocked doors.

To read my words, is to travel alongside my blood stream to
the depth of my brain,
The bound I share with words is like the connection ink has
with paper.

Upon white sheets creating verses that elevates, stimulate and
accumulates through brain waves.

So through my mind set, I give props to imagination painting pictures, not with a paintbrush but with a ball pen.

With words as my knowledge to inspire,
My tool as my pen to make permanent,
The letters that flow like a river of fishes, shall always be the net off my God given talent.

All black

They say am black . . .
So I say am proud
But they gaze at me with a funny look in their eyes like am neither human nor animal.

Many names I've been called and I try to ignore
Yet those ignorant words they spray at me, every time their sight catches mine sticks to me and I flow with tears.

The night brings nothing but calmer and I alone blend in like shadows in the shades.

Those who stop and stare with their twitching eyes speak in tongues I cannot understand, but reeks with words of filth and dirt.

Sometimes the mirror reflects the truth and looking back at me brings more than comfort but recognition.

So when they do ask what makes you, YOU?!
I close my eyes and let the words that bring me joy, flow down my tongue and speak the truth . . . Am all BLACK and that's who I am.

The stars

The sun,
The moon,
The stars,
The sun shines from above,
Yet always sets upon the sparkling tear drops of a shooting
star.

To wish upon a star
Is to wish upon a wishing well,
You see the stars that shine, is not the stars that glow

But the stars that glow are diamonds in the dirt
See the grey moon light up the purple skies,
And witness its true beauty with each spark.

Gaze upon the glorious skies,
And there lies the true wonders of our gorgeous planet Earth.

After dark

After dark, silence walks among the silent streets like a ghost whisperer.

The mystifying night can be as peaceful like the glowing moon, sometimes I hear the whispers of the night as I lay my head to sleep like a baby in its court.

Only in dreams can I witness the glorious glow of the sun rise, with no sight to glare at the visions of daylight.

Watching darkness spark with diamonds that shine makes the dark more memorable with all its mystery.
After dark!!

The echo of foxes footsteps still imprinted along the roadside, while morning arrives in its freshness of snow to pave a new day, and after dark no longer exist among sunlight.

The enchanted lady

The enchanted lady
A nightly vision of beauty
She moves and dance in a motion of slowness like a turtle on
the move.

Human eyes as naked as mine can only watch and admire from
a distance,
Because to shut thou sight, no longer will I bear witness to her
glow.

Oh her red lips bleeds the captions of a red, red rose sprung
between the soils of June.
Oh I shall ask once more, have you set eyes upon the enchanted
lady who stole my sight with her beauty?

In my eyes alone she walks and sways like a waving flower,
true in its natural fragrant and by name enchanted as a lady.

Dream

Dear dearest friend,

I know word's has not departed our lips in 365 days, yet last night was a dream among dreams.

For my naked skin has never embraced nakedness in private, but only in dreams.

Thoughts that float in mind can't seem to neglect the first attraction,
And affection that brought the magnetism and chemistry that sparked like fire.

Sleepless nights keeps me day dreaming of all that we sheared between sheets and conversations exchanged with words that roll from tongue.

When morning arrives and daylight catches my smile, I recollect the dream that kept me up till the sunshine brought day between the windows of my eyes.

Although I can't seem to replay back such a night, it's no longer a dream among dreams but reality that truly exist, and forever shall remain permanent till I rest in peace.

Prisoner of war

This system . . .
Is not truthful, nor faithful
Loyalties don't bear its name among men of government.

Your country NEEDS YOU!
So we pledge our aligns to our country,
The flag that fly high above water, we cherish and salute.

On the battle ground, we no longer men of society but a tool
for our country
And seen as heroes to the nation we swore to defend.

Morning sun rise, sun set, sun fall
Gun raves in its distance cries of terror, as bullets flickers among
nights stars like fireworks.

Children among many men shiver in fear, as sounds of bombs
rain down and plant their destruction upon earth's soil.

Civilise civilians caught between cross fires beyond enemy lines,
Body bags lay to rest alongside rotten decaying bodies as
blossoming poppies begin to bloom.

Deadly black smoke collides with the skies, intoxicating the
purified clouds with poisonous fumes.

A prisoner's war is its worst nightmare,
A soldier's fight is beyond the battle field but the nightly visions
of the dead.

Trapped within the nightly torments of cries,
Screams become the only voice that hunts the lonely mind.

A soldier's prize is to endure such pain, only to survive an
endless war and receive a badge to claim a hero's welcome.

Snow oh snow

Snow, oh snow
Snowflakes stain the chilly cold winds that whisper in the midnight hour.

The green of all grass, no longer visible beneath the blanket shades of white froth,
Snow oh snow.

It falls between the clouds, yet it settles upon the hard pavements and rest in perfect peace, like hibernating bears on icy snow plates.

Oh snow, that descend shall soon melt like raindrops, fade back into clouds and the circle of life continues.

Snow oh snow that stains the chilly cold winds beneath the nights stars brings a silent calmer with every sprinkle.

Emotions

Emotions are without its description,
Like a picture imitating its captions of depiction

Never been motionless, for my heart spill blood 'daily' like oil
floating in circulation

Am not motionless, for I feel pain as much as an animal, in my
eyes when sadness becomes a factor tears do rain like a stormy
night

My pride holds me grounded
My emotions keep me sane
My state of mind drives me crazy,
Yet there's a method to my sanity

There's no emotion, without the notion to let lose, for the
very emotion that cries out for freedom, is the same that seeks
recognition.

Watch them

We watch them fade

We watch them and watch them till our eyes bleed with tears, no longer are we tearful of salty tears.

These are our children, so let's gaze upon them with our watery eyes and shed down the knowledge of wisdom, passed down by our fore fathers.

Never letting them fly without wings, for they shall flop down and sink deeper than the deep blue sea.

Let's watch over them like the sun bears its shine upon our homeland
Let's protect them with both hands, love them dearly with our beating heart and never to let them fear the hands that feeds them.

Neglect them and the narrow corner shall inflict their weak emotions with fear
These are our children, because in their eyes is a caption of innocence so let's watch them.

Watch them grow bolder than life and up hold the bravery of a warrior.

Lend them their space for exploration is the mind-set of a child, so watch them.

Air my life

To breathe air in my lung is to inhale water like a fish.

If I had wings among wings, I shall be the eagle soaring high,
For the skies has never been the limit, but the fortress in which
our path of success lies

When raindrops fall in single droplets, they sink faster than the
eye could see.
So lend me the eyes of an owl, to glare upon the tear drops of
heaven.

If my ears do ring with sounds, let it share the sweet melody
of a hamming bird. Yet the notion of my lips is to bear the
sweetness of all delights.

My tongue has never been sneaky like a sneaky snake, but
with the venom of inspiring words.

The air we breathe is a gift of life, the water we drink has never
been thicker than blood. So when I do breathe, I inhale water
like a fish.

My only survival, air my life.

Goodbye!

Goodbye!

Goodbye to the ink within my pen
Goodbye to the strings to my shoes

Goodbye!

Goodbye to the moon as it fades among daylight,
Goodbye to the rhythm of my heart as I no longer exist in reality,
So goodbye to the world, for I shall never bear witness to the glow of the sun.

Nor will my hand ever touch the softness of a woman's bosom, nor will my lips kiss the softness of my fair ladies lips.

Without sight to see the world, darkness shall be the only comfort my lonely soul will embrace in moments of comfort.

Whispering goodbye along the echoing sounds of the wind brings back a pipe line of memories.

Goodbye

The need

The need to life is the need to air
For I need air like my lungs need gas, so I breathe daily.

I need you in more ways than one
Because my heart no longer beats in sync, as you are the only
rhythm that sings my instrument in perfect harmony.

So I need you now, not a second later for yesterday was never
an option, nor will I live long enough to see tomorrow.

I need you . . .

The colour

The colour . . .

Not the colour purple but the colours of skin and the colours of sight.

What colours do you describe to be?
Could you be black like me, brown like them or white like they . . . ?

Bear witness to the mirror in which your reflection shares the same tone as your own, and there you shall appear . . . the colour.

What skin must be shed to portray the layers of colours that we all bear beneath the sun?

Am neither the colours of a colourful rainbow, for the tone of my skin is not part of green, yellow, blue or red?
Nor am I the shade under an oak tree, for you see am described to be a BLACK MAN!

A weddings vow

Wedding day a question was once asked . . .
Do you take thee to be your lawful wife, to love and promise
to cherish and adore till death do you part?

I promise for I do have never been words of loyalty but
dishonesty, misery and divorce.

So I promise to love thee with all my heart and might.

I promise to protect her at all cost and never let any harm
infuse her mind or body.

Making promises has always been vowels I shall endlessly make,
for a man to make a promise must be kept and fulfilled.

So I promise to make each day a dream come true, I promise to
make each day sprinkle and sparkle with delight like diamonds
at night.

If ever I make a promise to my dear wife, I shall do all that
I can to make such a promise come true, because a promise
made is a promise kept.

I promise, I promise, for these are my vowels!

Words of 5

<u>Blemishes</u>
<u>Concrete</u>
<u>Salvation</u>
<u>Alight</u>
<u>Blue</u>

Upon the grounds of <u>concrete</u> from which <u>blemishes</u> of our history bears its roots.

<u>Salvation</u> beyond heavens gates shower upon our foreheads, more like a blessing of raindrops during dry season.

As the sky open up its <u>blue</u> ray, spring time crackle between broken concretes and only roses of innocents shall blossom.

Yet beneath these cracks, cries of forgiveness can be head elevating between the shattered soils.

Yet if hell can scream out in pain, then the punishment of flames are weapons of cleansing inflicted upon sinners soul set <u>alight.</u>

Dear diary

Dear diary,
Confessions of words shall conceive between these lines and hold so much thoughts and emotions.

You see the secrets we shed between sheets, are pieces of our souls we don't wish to share with no one but ourselves.

As a sinner like all men, I can truly say these eyes has laid sight to rotting black roses but also the beauty of blossoming sun flowers.

Only you stand out among the rest, for she shines brighter than the stars that glow, like a diamond among stars she's an angel with wings.

Pretty smiles,
Her crackling laugh,
Tears that pour when she no longer bears witness to the sun's glow, flows down in fast motion

Although every day is another day, it's never the same across the globe because the sun may fall on green grass but white clouds will fall on white slates.

Diary, when these eyes shed tears of salt, I close my twines and pray to God to replace these tears with flakes of snow.

We all enjoy the sight of white powder rather than the flooded rain.

Let's take it back to pretty smiles, crackling laugh, and diamonds from above.

She is the star fleeing the lonely space as my shooting star; her heart shall sit upon my love finger in the form of a ring.

A connection will form like two magnets attracted to one, as the future will be like the sun waiting to shine during day.

Yet if there be storms, rain or pain, then together we shall perceiver in any weather.

Mirror

There's a mirror in your eye
The magnification and symmetry that splits beauty from ugliness

There's your personality that flourish the aura of your glare, such intimidation is a caption that grows its roots from the tips of the devils hair . . .

Never been grown from perfection but there are flashes of perfection that glades from your tongue like the smoothness of ink, splashed in words of fiction

But there's the mirror that stares at you from the glow of the sun and the sparks in the night, it belongs with you as much as your shadow walks with you

Solitude is the only emptiness that allows loneliness to capture your tears,
But the image in the mirror conquers all hopes and hears all whispers in the dark!

Fear the sight of your bodily scars, for it is the pain that cut deeper than the shaper's of blades

See clear the truth in its purest and shed more tears beyond the leakage of a waterfall

Watch the splashes imitate the transparency of a clear crystallized glass and peak through the soul of a shy child.

Graveyard

Graveyard is nothing but grave stones,
Six feet deep is a pile of bones.

The flesh of man and the beauty of a lady blend among earth,
in history and in perfect collaboration.

The stench of flesh no longer exists in the world of living but
merely bonding with the roots.

Graveyard is nothing but grave stones, and the casket in which
the body rot
Is a gift to be judged or burn in hell!

You're beauty pt.1

Your name alone resembles poetry in its rhythmic form

Your smile I adore with every sight, with your laugh brings goose bumps upon my skin like a rush.

In your presence I blush in secrecy because am infatuated by your glow
I can't help but wish to merge my lips with your own.

Perfection may not walk with me like my shadow and neither are you . . .

But you do bear that special gift that makes the stars jealous to shine,
You are beauty in its natural state, like the mere caption of perfection in its prime.

She

Dedicated to mother

She's a goddess in disguise
Her soft dark hair and sparkling eyes shines at night like a twinkling star

She is by name the discovery of beauty at first sight, rear than undiscovered galaxies, like a star she glows with attraction

In a family of beauty she walks among prestige like a princess, wears a crown like a queen and upon red carpets she's treated like the stars.

Prayer

Imprint your knees in the presence of God
Bow down your head, and wipe away all falling tears.

Shut down your eyes as you gaze upon the heavenly
kingdom;
Embrace both palms as one and voice out your sins.

Speak and he shall listen,
Pray and he may reply,
Confess and he shall sweep away all wrong.

A prayer, 'NO', more like a letter to the Holy Father.

Attraction

If only I could remember that first day, first hour, that very moment that butterflies took flight within my stomach

Recollecting the smile and sparkling eyes that conquered my heart in a matter of minutes

Sometimes I sit back and reminisce on the attraction that brought my tongue to lose speech and eyes to glow wide

Questions I ask myself consciously, was the night silent or cold with winter's breeze?

That alone makes me wonder was there ever a full moon or just her glow shining bright beneath the star lights?

A day of attraction or just emotions misunderstood by her mere beauty in my eyes?

Sometimes I feel my thoughts alone plays mini tricks with the emotions that circulates in my head,

And yet she got me puzzling with the one night of attraction and provoking my eyes to watch her every move.

Am I attracted to her or just her curvy figure in which her soul has taken refuge?

The very questions that got my mind circulating are the ones'
that got my emotions bubbling with chemistry

Am attracted to her attraction and the very posture in which
she walks, the very lips so sweet with tender kiss and in her
eyes glittering with sparkling glow.

The story

Impossible is without its possibilities!
So I dare not speak what cannot be said
For thy tongue has lost sight of speech.

Behind these double vision of sight that allows me to glare through the foot steps of a past left behind . . . there's a childhood story untold.

Named after a king, yet unknown to his last name and a voice continues to echo "who are you?"

Constant dreams of a place unseen, untouched by these very hands, embrace the hope of belonging.

A mother to a child that bears no bloodline, yet embraced by a family who bears no relations but the comfort of a loving family

On the tip of his tongue, the beat of his heart rested the very expressions he feared to let lose, so as night falls and he lays his head to sleep . . .

The very words that shy away from light, foams into tears and roll down his cheeks as it rest upon the mat

Flood of tears explodes from this fragile body as it spills from dream to realities door mat

Within these eyes sat a lost boy filled with sadness, yet with no
shoulder to absorb the very pain and anger bottling up inside

A mothers love and unknown father with settlement in a far, far
land a waits to reunite.

Dreams do come true for as time walked by, 99.9% of blood
certified to prove, blood is thicker than water.

Reunited as one,
The very streams that gave him life,
A mother to a father,
A father to a son,
And the bound of brothers, united as a family.

Raised as a child, matured as a boy and achieved as a man, the
past shapes you, the present is now and the future is as you
plan.

Mistakes

Mistakes are made to be forgiven
Mistakes must be a man's middle name

Our treasured jewels are our main downfall, it uplifts at the first sight of an attractive female

The path that leads to unfaithful is where our curiosity takes us and yet with each mistake made we must learn from

Although repetition is the father of learning, mistakes must not be repeated it must be cast aside and embrace faithful and loyalty as a companion!

Expression

Life is a dream
And night after night,
I dream of loving a stolen heart
A moment spent with you, is a dream that has made reality its
goal

Seems like seconds has come to past since your words made an
echo with my dreams and time no longer walks in slow-motion
but walks alongside my shadow like a loyal friend

My skin catches cold like flies caught in a web and only 'you',
can cast aside this cold and bring back the heat like boiling
kettle

There are feelings within that surface like a volcanic eruption
and continue to grow in rapid speed, for you alone . . . they
will flow for miles and never sleep till death extinguish my very
heart beat

Such expression of deep thoughts comes straight from the very
depth of my rhythmic drum beat, delivering the very emotions
that makes me smile, makes me cry and make me laugh with
love.

A lie . . .

To deceive is a crime
Punishable by guilt
Through the words that misleads shall lead to expressions of truth

If I am to be a liar,
Then am guilty for the verbal lies I have committed and for truth be told I must allow the truth to set me free

To receive forgiveness I must bear shame and embrace the word 'sorry', because the lies that has rolled off my unworthy tongue needs to be cast to shame!

A lie . . .

Betrayal

Am a sinner for the things I have committed
My only hope is to seek forgiveness
Never did I wish to fall into the devils trap of temptation and
flirtation

As I kneel down in disgrace pleading and seeking for forgiveness,
I sit back speechless and without words to speak

Silence begins to walk among the very room that breaths life
through my lungs, and the music to my heart echo's in my ears
like a drum roll

If words could describe the actions that led my lips to betrayal
another . . .

Each sentence will implement the very tears that break the
barriers of my eyes.

My own promises broken by the very lips that brought it life, I
feel like dirt trembled on by those faithful.

Trapped in fear of my own actions and my only way out is to
be set free and introduced to the light of loyalty.

Unbelievable

Unbelievable!
Yet you believe me, so why deceive me
When I have buried my faith in you like religion.

Don't mistake these tears for weakness, they simply spilling on the thought of your betrayal.

The mere confusion displayed on your face alerts me your mind is contemplating on your actions

Emotions on display, but I can't pass judgement so my brain wave articulates punishment.

Your eyes will bleed in tears,
Your hair will fall in disgrace,
The very tongue that speaks will no longer bear fruit to speech
The very beauty my heart fell in love, will crumble and blown to dust!

Time will fade, my eyes will cry and the pieces to my heart crumbling will soon break to puzzles and wait once again to be mended.

But the very memories that brought us joy, along with the rain and stormy nights will always be days that will R.I.P.

Mirror, mirror

There's a reflection in the mirror
I dare not ask its name, so I watch it watch me like an owl
watching the night's stars

Lips with movement, yet words cannot be heard through his
vocal cords, so with ears to hear, I creep closer to let the sound
vibrate the rhythmic beat in the air

A question mirrored the very movements of his lips and asked,
"Can you live without the very ears that embrace sounds?"

A blunt expression began to reflect and imitate a sense of focus,
contemplating on the very words asked . . .

You see without ears to hear the very sounds that make my
heart sing, drum a beat in its rhythmic flow like a river that
flows for miles . . .

Nothing can be heard but the wind from which the very words
spoken vibrate between airwaves like sonic.

The very reflection mirroring the symmetry of my expression
is a depiction of all the emotions bottled up in my memory
bank.

Mirror, mirror on my wall inform me of my deep fears as I stare
through the windows of my soul.

Choice

They gave us a choice, to live or to die?
We made no promises to sacrifice the very life that brought us
love and pain
So patience became a virtue

Who are they to give us the choice to decide; to end a life that
was once blessed by GOD is dishonesty and the evil that planted
such a seed will rot in the very pit that consumes guilt

To jump will be a choice made by me, and yet the very fear
that's got my heart racing stops me from taking such a leap

So what's a man on death row to do? If the choice is truly mine,
then a choice has to be made!

To jump to be free from solitude, to live or to die?

"Treat me good"

"Treat me good" she said, with tiny droplets of diamonds escaping her visions of sight

They say the eyes are the windows to the soul, so we mirror each other's reflection in moments of exchanging words

Tears fall, but tears do dry and sadness can always be replaced by happiness
Give me the chance to share with you the very emotions that makes my heart jump

Lend me your hands
Let's walk with time
Let's talk and joke about moments gone past

From the beginning we made no promises to make forever a reality, only to let loyalty, honesty, trust and love is the guide to our compass

So when I do make mistakes, never forget I am a man by gender with the very blood stream that streams from 'Adam' running through my veins

"Treat me good"
Then "honey, treat me well" for I too deserve the very respect that you demand . . .

Some women wish to be treated like a queen, but not willing to treat a man like a king.

We have touched each others soul, completed a puzzle to perfection and yet we have walked among tears, wake up with a glimpse of morning sun only to watch the blue skies invaded by grey clouds

As much as we seek for bright light, "good times", summer always comes by the season
Cold spells, chilly nights and wet skies always reflect winters blues

"You have changed" she said with a mist of sadness mirroring her face (pause).

Changed?
Seasons change by the monthly as much as you flow with droplets of red spots when time of the month approaches

Our life may not run with perfection, but we sail through the ups and the down like sea waves, no days are the same.

Can't change, won't change, not changed
For my emotions may not slide free through the wind, but alongside you the very empty hole that used to be filled with tears has mended

"Treat me good" she says . . .
Have I not been there when raindrops fled the very sparkle in your eyes?

It's true, there are days arguments become a frequent misunderstanding,
But never have I struck you in anger nor degraded your womanhood in anyway . . .

Your heart alone beats alongside mine like a drum roll, your hands alone has nurtured me from the moment I said "I do" so treat me good.

In the event of my demise

If I was to die today,
Let the last tears that fall down my cheek spark with love

In the event of my demise, let my final words spark with truth
and seek out forgiveness

Will my heart bleed in pain or will I suffer in darkness?

To die a young age, will my soul ever rest in peace or will my
bodily pieces be donated as donations?

When judgement has been passed, where will my floating soul
rest in peace?

Is there a place for young souls beyond the afterlife of death or
is death unsettling as much as life is unpredictable?

Will my final words of truth ever reach the ears of my loved
once or will it all fade in the mist of night?

Will I cry along with the tears from the skies stirring down the
barrel of a pistil?

Should I fear death at the final scene or should I look forward
to the heavenly promises of a good life?

At the end of life will I be led down the steps of heaven or will
I encounter the devil in disgust along the chambers of hell?

Lips with lips

Let lips do what hands do best, kiss with each touch

My lips stand in stillness awaiting the touch of a ladies lip, so let thou lips travel across the very airwaves that I breathe . . .

As it floats among lands let it land on your very lips that u speak with.

So let thy lips rest on thy lips so I can wear the very lipstick painted on your lips . . .

Let lips do what hands do best, let's kiss if not then let lips touch to taste the sweetness of each lips

Let's do lips to lips, forget CPR all I seek is the chemistry of fusion between two chemically active elements

Please read my lips like a bed time story, as it depicts the very romantic gestures of a Shakespeare novel.

Mentality

Mind my state of mind
Don't label my behaviour as crazy
The very emotional struggle that these tears may display is a
past long left behind . . . so no am neither mad!

Don't judge me with the very eyes that judges you

For our lives bears no link, am simply interested in the attention
your ears has on offer and the very knowledge that you possess

Lend me your ears to listen to the conflict that's inflicted by the
voices echoing in mind

Hear these words that flee my trembling lips as I contemplate
and express the pieces that are yet to be solved

Assess my situation, yet make no pre judgement to my bodily
language . . . am simply anxious

All I seek is these words that travel from my lips to meet with your
ears and listen to the very problems that's got me confused

Help me make sense of the voices penetrating my brain waves
for I can't seem to think straight

Give me the information to enable me to progress from this
depression over shadowing my livelihood

Encourage me to live a full life or with these voices as my command
will rest in a casket and no longer exist in this dimension!

Ride

In a train ride with no driver,
My destination determined by every stop, am a worm beneath this cities tunnels with no sight to set alight a clear flash of what's at the end of the tunnel.

Lend me a flash light to see through the dark, for this little candle needs a match to set it ablaze

Can I see if I cannot see, with these eyes wide open blurred in vision . . . could I be lost or my destination unknown?

Should I scream help or allow the wet tears running down my cheeks lead me towards the river bank . . .

HELP, HELP, HELP . . . but my voice is yet to break so I scream like a pig in pain.

Without the very legs or wings to take flight, am struck by fear, impaired by speech as my blurred vision runs with blood.

This is neither a ride of life nor a state of mind, but realities nightmare's that comes as a ride.

Name

She gave me a name, one that I did not ask for, but gave me a name I am now known by

They gave me a name, "man" the very gender that allows me to create and despise the seeds that reproduce in nine months

They gave me a name, I could not believe, for I can never see my self as the rat sleeping between unknown sheets, "one night stand"

Sometimes they stain me with words used in the past that no longer implies with the same reference "nigga", so I embrace it as the nature of my clan

We all born from the same gender, "women" the lord blessed them for they truly the chosen one's, we the seeds that lay the roots and watch it grow from a baby to a child

They gave as a name that we now live by, so if any one asks what's your name?

Remember your mother for she gave birth and blessed you with a name.

Nothing

Nothing comes from nothing
Boredom arrives out of nothing
Push comes to shave, the nails will be sharp

Too cool for cool
But not uncool to be moody, just a factor of emotion

Smoke free for your lungs is in need of air
Enter when door opens but never forget to pull
Excitement always elevates when the mood is always right
Important is a factor, so support when tears fall from a friend's
eye

Forget sex
Forget drugs
Forget negativity
And embrace life to the fullest

Nothing may come from nothing, but to seek out everything is
to be in competition with your self!

Poor man

We were poor,
As poor as poor can be
We worked the land like slave workers picked up cotton
There were days meaning to life never made no sense

The hand that fed us, were the very hands that planted the very
seeds that brought us food

There were days raindrops never blessed the land, our cattle's
walked around like zombies

Our bear feet stains the ground like foot soldiers matching
through deserted deserts

Four seasons!
Never did rainfall bless our dry land
Poverty becomes reality when a man can't feed his spouse

So it's true what they say . . .
"He's a poor man with land the size of Texas, with cattle's in
their thousands, but not a puddle of rain in sight"

These bear hands with these bear feet
No clothing, for clothing is materialistic for those that can afford
On my skin is the very nature that wears me

Fatherly love were the very hands that thought us
Motherly love came with hugs and kisses

Am a poor man with a poor sight
Strong hands reflecting hard work
Strong bones imitating strong legs, with a tough skin, so no
goose bumps

Enriched by the very land my feet walks on, and yet poor
enough to hunt to survive
Am a poor man, with a poor heart but I don't live for me, I live
for life.

Witness

Witness life in its reality
Dreams alone could not despise the very souls that cause grief

With eyes I watch the world in its misery, yet there are days I bear witness to beauty

Through the very windows of a lover's sight, the very windows of my soul captured tears pilling down her cheeks like natural waterfall

These tears did not deceive pain but gave birth to a new spark
A scream as loud as the big bang, took birth in its splendid form

As if the skies were rejoicing, thunder bloomed in a storm of claps and tears fell from grace among heavens rain like angels shedding droplets of joy

Speech therapy never fled the lips, but innocent cries echoed through the ear drums like a celebration, witnessed.

Who

Who are you?
Lately I ask myself who am I?

Can you for see the answers I search for daily?
Am not a lonely dog for am a cat who lost his way

Do I bear the adversity of a juvenile delinquent?
I could be, for I possess the posture of a twiching street corner
hustler.

My education don't bear witness to books or teachers, but
papers upon papers, upon papers

Standing alone between the street signs and the corner shops,
is like standing still within the assembly hall waiting to hand
over my paper

Am neither a lover to a natural born lady, but a fist hundler to
a woman beater

See am ignorant to the down right selfish things I commit, for
am so blinded by paper, upon paper, upon paper . . . that I
inhale the filth of dope

See my soul aren't corrupt by the streets I walk on daily, but
am trapped among the devils work of money motivation

Yet I seek out some love to set me free because as they say
"love shall set you free", with this in mind am on the journey
of pursueing the pursuit of happiness.

It's a shame I have never met love, for am lost among the jungle of a forest dealer

So you ask; who are you?

Well lately I ask, who am I?

You see among the nightly shadows I plead with God to send me a sign to set me free

My life hungs in limbo like a linched NIGGA, day after day my red blazing eyes bear witness to this ghetto life story like a movie screen

There's the mirror that watches me, within there's a lost soul searching for a greener grass on the land of dreams

Does that make me a dreamer, a searcher, or someone who seek for the love and happiness he never witnessed?

So I shall ask once more, who am I?
For I have never been told I bear a name or loved by those who share love . . .
So who are you?!

Questions with answers

What's life, without a dream to depict realities fantasies?

Dreamless!

What's a book without its sheets?

Empty!

What is an author without his pen?

State of mind, speech!

What's a man without a woman?

Lonely!

What's a woman without her make up?

Faceless!

What's a child without imagination?

Boredom!

The speech of I

Told you once:
"I aren't a painter, but I know how to connect with words like ink sleeps on paper"

To claim to be a poet you must love words like lips love lips 'kiss'

Told you once:
"I don't write, I simply rewrite what my mind says, like a book you don't read until it's written"

The speech of I is more than the speech of me
It is the journey through which my pen travels through the tunnels of my state of mind

You see, someone once told me:
"You got to fall to rise" and at the moment am rising above water, no longer sinking nor drowning but floating among high clouds

No longer am I a fractured child between cracks of incomplete, but a man with these hands imprinted upon books of knowledge

These very eyes set upon the path of success, no matter how high the mountain shall be . . .

The sky will never be the limit but the first goal to succeed!

The speech of I has always been the story that connects reality with dreams, never has it immitated non fiction nor has it portrayed the imagery of art.

The speech of I, are words that flow with emotion like a river that rise and falls, going through the motion.

Fame

Fame is more than a name
Fame is to be seen
Fame is to be heard
Fame is to be loved,
Adored by millions who chants your name, known by all, no longer an individual but living through captions of a lens

Reality don't exist in public, only behind close doors can one peel off fame and be recognised as an individual

Within the spotlight you're merely an idol of entertainment, a model in a funs eye and an element of tabloid story telling

To live among fame is to entertain, conqured by the stage, never to be part of the crowd but the envy of those who wish to be more like a celebrate

Fame will always be more than a name
Fame is to be seen
Fame is to be heard
Fame is to be loved adored by millions who chants your name
Known by all, no longer an individual but living through the windows of a lens

Kisses with words

If a kiss says what words can't, then allow me to use these lips as words to immitate my intentions.

Let's tango upon the dance floor and allow both feet to do the talking.

If a painting depicts a thousand words, then on your lips as my canvas, I shall paint you a vivid image.

See Picaso was a painter who worked with his hands, as for me am an artist who works with his lips.

If diamonds are forever, then kisses shall be everlasting moment that stops time in fusion.

If words are depiction of emotions then kisses imitates affection, lips with connection and together we bond kisses with words.

Words of advice

Dream a dream that's worth achieving,
Make a goal that's worth succeeding,
Live a life that's worth dying for

Make promises you will always for fill
And never let the tears you shed cause you pain, yet let it be
tears of joy

They say follow your heart but without state of mind to match,
doubt shall inflict the very decisions made.

So never forget to follow your heart but consult with mind and
never regret any decisions made.

Who am I?

I am a winner among many winners,
A fighter among all survivors,
I shall achieve what they said I couldn't
And overcome my worst of all failures.
I walk among many souls
Like angels on cloud nine,
For I too bear wings and fly like an eagle.
I could be a traveller, yet my destination unknown
For in this world, tomorrow may never come, so I dream.

I have a dream, not like Martin Luther,
But I too have a dream.
I dream of a better tomorrow,
A day that children lay down guns and knives
And shake hands like men, I dream!

I pray for those who have no hope,
For such a word has never come true, I dream!
I wish for those who are lost at war, to find their piece of home
and rest in peace, I dream!

For you see, I am a creature like all humans,
I bear a heart, a pair of eyes to see the world,
Two legs to walk on grass
And two hands to hold in hands.
You see I am no different from you, why? Because I have a
dream and so do you.

Flow

Flow!
There's a stream that my blood runs through
Like the flow of river running down river bank
Let it run like a runner on track, watching time tick in its seconds
like life in its breath, priceless.

Nothing like clockwork and when eyes meet light sight sees all
that reality has to offer, flow!

Tears fall from a mothers eyes only to meet a stream of flood
fleeing her daughters sight, splashes of tears falls from grace.

A chain reaction to a bond uplifted by the very grief they
endure, flow!

In life there comes moments that shears no reason to the very
reasons that we exist, so existence comes with millions of
questions, unanswered.

So when pain, fortune and love comes in times that can't be
explained, flow!

We live with one life
Speak with one tongue
Smell with one nose
Touch with two hands
And with legs alone we walk for miles.

Our journey meets with one promise; 'death' is inevitable so as
time ticks let it flow!

Flow with every day that rain falls from sky
Allow each drop to sink through your veins as a blessing.

Let ears ring with sounds on a daily bases, for repetition is the
father of learning.

Embrace lips with lips and shear hands with hands, let legs do
what they were born to do best . . . stand on your own two
feet, flow!

Lightning Source UK Ltd.
Milton Keynes UK
UKOW052015120412

190624UK00001B/39/P